To Michael, Ich liebe Dich ~ CF

For Matilda, with love ~ BC

SIMON AND SCHUSTER

First published in Great Britain in 2009 by Simon and Schuster UK Ltd
1st Floor, 222 Gray's Inn Road, London WC1X 8HB
A CBS COMPANY

A CIP catalogue record for this book is available from
the British Library upon request

ISBN: 978 1 84738 301 3 (HB)
ISBN: 978 1 84738 302 0 (PB)

Printed in China

7 9 10 8

Aliens in Underpants Save the World

Claire Freedman & Ben Cort

SIMON AND SCHUSTER

London New York Sydney

Aliens love underpants,
It's lucky that they do,
For pants helped save our universe,
Sounds crazy, but it's true!

On one pants-pinching mission,
As the aliens zoomed through space,
Their spaceships shook and wobbled,
Ooooh! Their hearts began to race.

Their radars bleeped, their sirens wailed,
On came the warning light!
Yikes! Heading straight for planet Earth,
Was one huge meteorite!

Meanwhile, on Earth, the scientists,
Had such an awful fright.
"What's THAT?" they gulped in horror,
"Picked up on our satellite?"

The fire engines came racing,
Police and air rescue too,
But with just four hours 'til impact,
There was little they could do!

Quick! Down to Earth the aliens shot,
And jumped out with a shout,
"No time to lose, if Earth blows up,
Our pants supply runs out!"

They took pants down from washing lines,
And raided knicker stores,
They sneaked inside our houses,
And pulled bloomers out of drawers.

The aliens stitched the underwear,
And proudly they unfurled,
The most GINORMOUS pair of pants,
Made in the whole wide world!

Wheee! Whizzing in their spaceships,
They stretched out the pants in place,
And as the meteor landed – PING!
It zoomed back into space!

"The meteorite has vanished!"
Gasped the people in surprise,
"We thought we saw huge underpants,
But can't believe our eyes!"

Back home the aliens all cheered,
"Our pants plan was fantastic,
We saved the Earth and underpants,
With pingy pants elastic!"

So should your pants go missing,
There's no need to make a fuss,
Let the aliens have their fun
They've done SO much for us!